MW01057043

# ALL YOUR RACIAL PROBLEMS WILL SOON END

## The Cartoons of Charles Johnson

**New York Review Comics**

**A Work from the Johnson Construction Co.**

THIS IS A NEW YORK REVIEW COMIC
PUBLISHED BY THE NEW YORK REVIEW OF BOOKS
435 Hudson Street, New York, NY 10014
www.nyrb.com/comics


A catalog record for this book is available from The Library of Congress.

Cover design by Alexandra Zsigmond.

New York Review Comics would like to thank Dan Nadel for his significant role in the creation of this book.

ISBN: 978-1-68137-673-8

Printed in South Korea

10 9 8 7 6 5 4 3 2 1

# Table of Contents

Black Humor
by
Charles R. Johnson
JOHNSON PUBLISHING COMPANY, INC.
$3.95
.615

NOTES
FROM
THE PAD

# From High School to *Black Humor* (1965 – 70)

Like many if not most cartoonists, I've been drawing constantly since childhood. Drawing and looking at visual art was all I wanted to do during elementary school. I remember spending whole afternoons blissfully seated before a three-legged blackboard my parents got me for Christmas, drawing until my knees and the kitchen floor beneath me were covered with layers of chalk, and the piece in my hand was reduced to a wafer-thin sliver. My art (and later literature) classes were the ones where I came alive.

By the time I entered high school, I was hungering to publish anywhere as a cartoonist. I took a two-year cartooning course with Lawrence Lariar, who was the cartoon editor of *Parade* magazine, the *Best Cartoons of the Year* books, and the author of over one hundred titles, including detective fiction that he wrote under a couple of pseudonyms. By the time I finished his course, I was publishing illustrations for the catalog of a magic company in Chicago as well as stories and cartoons in my high school newspaper, *The Evanstonian*. One of the panel cartoons I drew, as well as a comic strip called *Wonder Wildkit* that I did with a friend, each won a second-place award for high school cartoonists in a national contest sponsored by the Columbia Graduate School of Journalism. The full-page cartoon that appears on page ten was in the last issue of *The Evanstonian* the spring I graduated.

**'Our ancestors called this a Homecoming Queen'**

In 1966, I went off to college at Southern Illinois University as a professional cartoonist and illustrator, majoring in journalism. As soon as I hit campus, I got hired as a cartoonist for the school newspaper, *The Daily Egyptian*, and spent the next four years churning out every sort of drawing and two comic strips, *The God Squad* and *Trip*, for its pages. Not long after that, I was hired as an editorial cartoonist for the local newspaper, *The Southern Illinoisan*, where I worked part-time after graduation as a reporter and columnist to support work on my master's degree in philosophy.

During my college years, my work became so increasingly radical that one faculty advisor to *The Daily Egyptian* asked me to stop doing the cartoons in which I was calling for revolution. In the summer of 1969, I did an internship at *The Chicago Tribune*, writing copy and drawing illustrations (the King Kong drawing) for their public service "Action Express" column. By that time, I had completed the manuscript for my first book, *Black Humor*. I put together *Black Humor* at the same time that I was hosting a how-to-draw show called *Charlie's Pad* for the PBS station WSIU-TV, which was broadcast nationally. *Black Humor* was done in a furious week of drawing when I cut my classes after attending a reading by black nationalist poet Amiri Baraka, who, during the Q&A, told black students in the audience to take their talents back to the black community. The title *Black Humor* resonates with not only the idea of humor involving black

**Will we let a test score ruin her education experience?**

THE EVANSTONIAN PRESENTS A PICTORIAL RESUME OF THE SCHOLASTIC YEAR 1965-66 — IF YOU CAN'T FIND YOURSELF ON THIS PAGE — THEN YOU'RE JUST NOT "IN"!!
SWAMP GAS
SCRIPT
CENSORED
KARATE + JUDO MADE EASY
WHO ARE ALL THESE PEOPLE ?!!
ETHS PUBLICATIONS
VENI VIDI VI
HASTY HEART
YAMO
MOD FOR-EVER
EVANSTONIAN
WORD MOSIACS
AQUETTES '66
REPEAL STUDENT DAY!!!
DRAFT NOTICE 1-A
SENIOR CLASS MOVIE
LOLITA
WURDS
CENTRAL COUNCIL
MEETING IN PROGRESS
ZZ ZZZ!
PROM
DADDY + DAUGHTER DINNER DANCE
CHAS. JOHNSON '66

people, but also the other meaning "black humor" has, i.e., humor that, like gallows humor, jokes about serious and often depressing topics.

After finishing it, I had no idea where to send it. Fortunately, I showed it to Bob Cromie, the book editor at the *Tribune*, who suggested I walk it down Michigan Avenue to Johnson Publications, which published *Ebony*, *Jet*, and *Black World*, the magazines where I would soon be publishing single-panel gag cartoons. Johnson Publications' publisher, John H. Johnson, liked the book and immediately took it—I remember shaking his hand when I returned to their offices, and him telling me which cartoons he enjoyed the most.

Looking at this cartoon collection fifty-three years after its creation, I'm reminded of how liberated I felt during the week images and ideas came pouring out of me. I felt my imagination had been given permission to go anywhere, that no limits constrained me, as they did when I was doing political cartoons for, say, *The Southern Illinoisan*, a newspaper that, like all newspapers, had a specific political orientation. With *Black Humor*, on the other hand, my imagination felt free, as if its own Juneteenth had arrived. As an artist, the experience was exhilarating for me. These were no longer just "assignments" I did for others as a cartoonist. It didn't feel like hack work. No, during that week it felt like pure fun. Like the exuberant play I remembered having on that blackboard in my parent's kitchen. Some of that same wild spirit carried over, I guess, into my first three published novels, *Faith and the Good Thing*, *Oxherding Tale*, and *Middle Passage*, and into recent short stories like the sci-fi fabliau "Guinea Pig" in my story collection *Night Hawks*.

I think a good deal of that intense week's work still has resonance, and a certain satiric punch about race relations, which in many ways have not changed in the last fifty-two years, and perhaps never will.

***George Washington Carver, are you wasting time again?***

***Rufus Junior!*** ***Johnny!***

***I like you, you're different.***

**Free at last!**

***How dare you be an idealist?***

***Is it that bad in the ghetto?***

***One hundred books of matches?***

***Integration? Hell No.***
***The only way to freedom***
***is through complete segregation.***

***Show me a black integrationist***
***and I'll show you an Uncle Tom.***

***Yah! Rap on, Brother.***
***We hear ya!***

***How'd it go tonight, Tom?***

WASHINGTON
DETROIT
WATTS
CLEVELAND

***He's cute. Does he picket yet?***

CBS
FREEDOM NOW
WHITE POWER

***I can lick any liberal in the house!***

***Jackson, when you find the time, I'd like to see you in my office.***

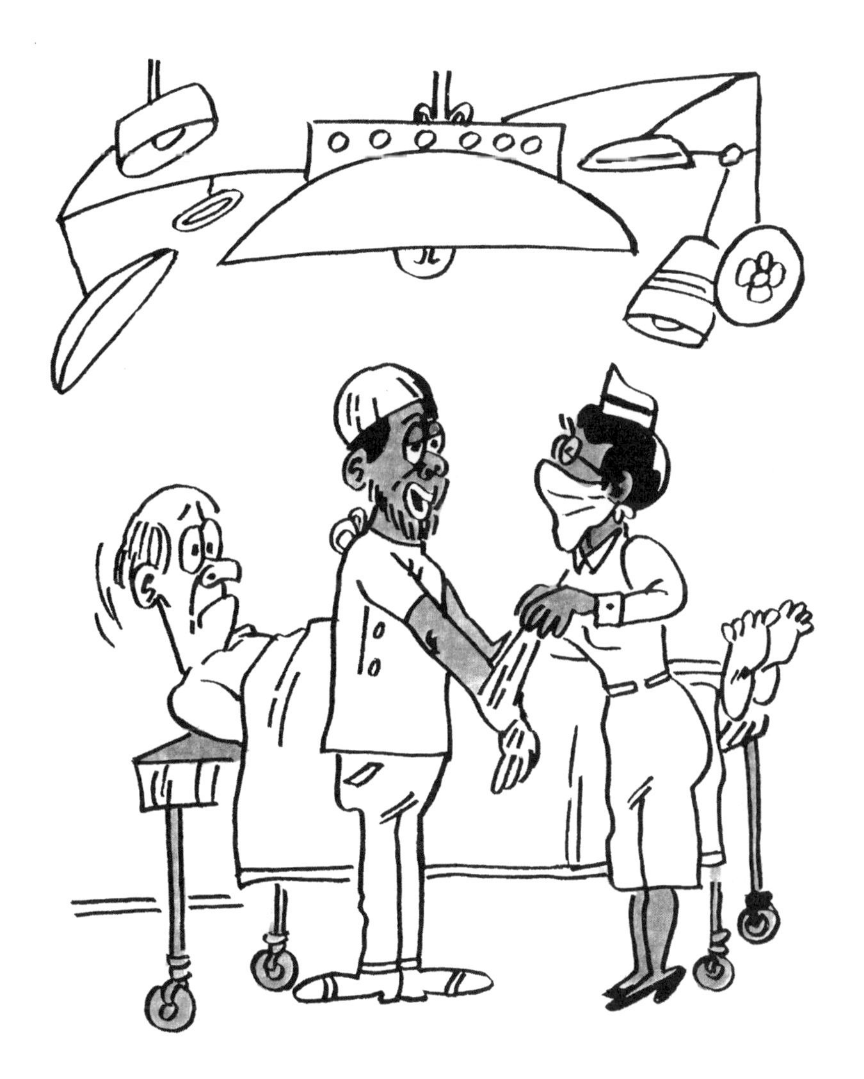

***Muhammad was right. White devils must be eliminated.***

***Psst, he's a mulatto . . . pass it on.***

***Here's a good buy.***
***He was owned by a militant who only spoke Swahili.***

***But I never expected you to be sexually superior, dear.***

***From now on you can refer to me as "Friday X."***

**Be careful what you say to him.**

***Oops!***

COLORED
NEGROES
AFRO-AMERICANS
BLACKS
ONLY
WHITES ONLY

$2.50

AS-729511

# HALF-PAST NATION TIME

By Charles Johnson

# Half-Past Nation Time (1972)

*Half-Past Nation Time* is a cartoon collection that was and wasn't. It was published by Aware Press in California, a fly-by-night operation that disappeared right after sending me my author's copies. The publisher also did a Houdini with a cartoon manuscript I'd put together on slavery, *I Can Get Her for You Wholesale.* So, *Half-Past Nation Time* can only be found in the rare book section at some libraries. Fifty years later, the only copy I have is worn out and falling apart.

More than anything else, the drawings in *Half-Past Nation Time* reflect that in my early twenties I was, philosophically, a Marxist and a socialist. Along with such philosophical traditions as phenomenology and Eastern philosophy, Marxism was something new in academia in the 1960s, as was Black Studies—in 1969, I was one of ten student discussion leaders at Southern Illinois University for a big lecture course on Black Studies taught by black graduate students. (There were no black faculty members at the time on campus to teach such a course.) My master's thesis in 1973 was on the influence that Marx and Freud had on Wilhelm Reich's practice of psychiatry in the 1930s. A year later, when I was in the Ph.D. program in philosophy at Stony Brook University, the first class they assigned me to teach as a graduate student was titled "Radical Thought." In that course, I taught my students everything from Marx's 1844 Manuscripts to Chairman Mao's "Little Red Book." My immersion in radical thought is evident in the introduction to *Half-Past Nation Time*, where I wrote, "*Half-Past Nation Time* is about the time bomb ticking of evolution's clock; it is about black folks in search of new forms and symbols to serve as legitimate cultural developments and changes in the contour of society. It is about the surge of black nationalism that has reshaped America in its eleventh hour, the charcoal élan vital that injected new blood in the tired veins of Western culture [and about] . . . new bonds created by new men forming a new nation, laughing together with a new sense of humor."

Given my intellectual orientation in the early '70s, it should come as no surprise that I liked the original Black Panthers (and had a couple of friends who were in Illinois chapters of the Black Panther Party). They were dramatic, brash, Marxist, and oh so very visual with their berets, guns, and leather jackets. Their iconography was simply too rich for me, as a cartoonist, not to want to draw.

As things turned out, my early study and teaching of Marxist philosophy eventually fell away in my mid-twenties, replaced in my doctoral studies by a greater focus on continental philosophy (phenomenology) and literary aesthetics. And in my personal life, political radicalism was replaced by a deepening commitment to an even more radical (in my opinion) Buddhist practice. Its emphasis on non-duality, loving kindness (*metta*) toward all sentient beings, and constant examination of my own presuppositions, premises, assumptions, and prejudices through mindfulness training proved to be antithetical to Marxism.

*"I sure hope your aim is better when the revolution comes!"*

*"According to my calcuations, we can expect a revolution in this country around 2962 A.D."*

*"'Nation Time' wasn't exactly the answer I was looking for, Eddie."*

*"First, you must lower your psychological defenses."*

*"Thank God, Lucy, I made it through another week without making a racial commitment."*

*"How'd you guess that I painted it?"*

*"You'd be surprised how many people mistake me for H. Rap Brown."*

*"You can't raid our house now; the place is a mess!"*

*"That's what I like–a pusher who relates to the community and its needs."*

*“Really, Dad, I don’t think it went like this.”*

*"Can I interest you in a subscription to* Better Homes and Gardens*?"*

*"I suppose you're wondering why I've gathered you all here. . . "*

*"They really know how to hurt a guy, eh, Pop?"*

*"Support the community? If I'm elected of course I'll support the black community!"*

*"What's this I hear about the FBI taking an office right below ours?"*

*"You wanna talk about it, Leslie?"*

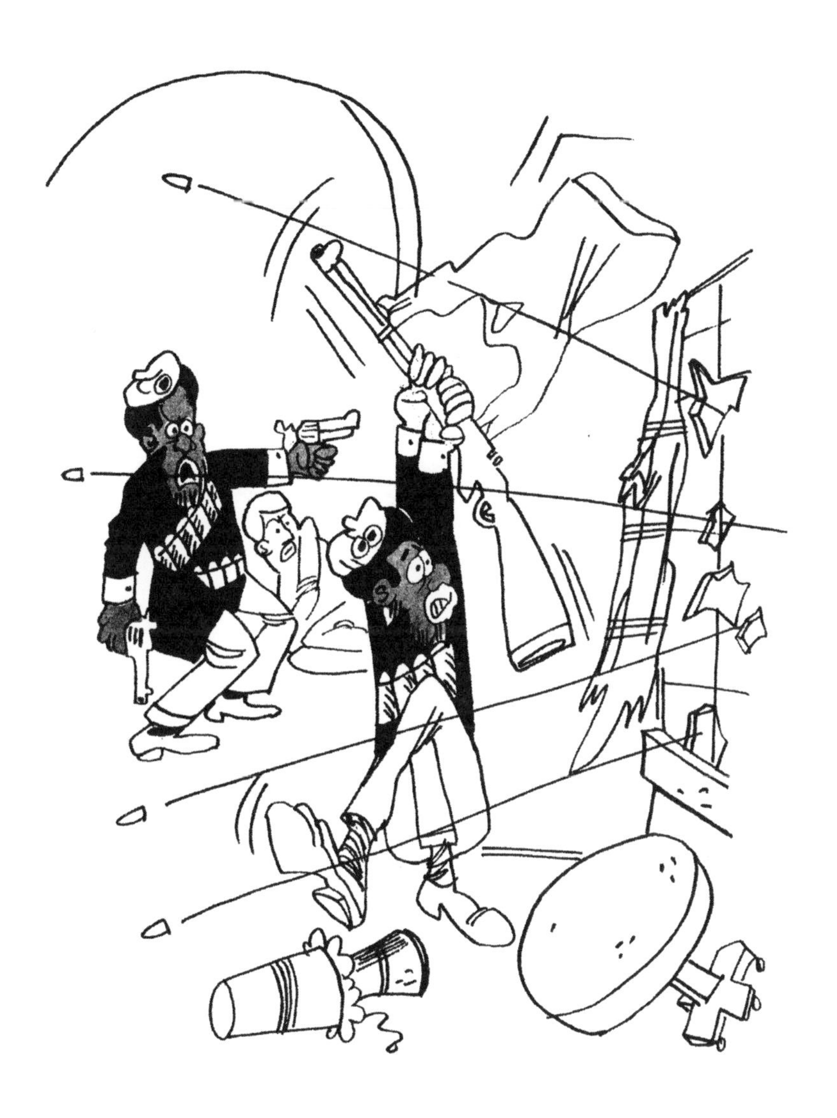

*"Jackson, come to my office right after this raid is over!"*

*"I wish you Black Panthers would change that sign."*

*"Doctor, how'd you like a place in our revolution as Minister of Science?"*

*"How many times must I remind you that we're involved in an economic and **not** a sexual revolution!"*

*"I think we're in luck."*

*"Nice touch, don't you think?"*

FANON
WRETCHED OF THE EARTH

*"But if we're **all** brothers and sisters, wouldn't it be incest if we got married?"*

*"Get out of my pocket."*

*“Check the style book before writing headlines, Smith.”*

*"But suppose he doesn't want a ticket to the 'Honor America Day' festivities?"*

*"Wow, what a gas–my fortune cookie says:*
*'The revolutionary people of China will follow*
*Chairman Mao in the destruction of the revisionist pigs.'"*

*"Any trouble with the police today, Johnny?"*

*"Hello. Station manager?"*

*"I won't forget this, fellas."*

*"There will never be another Minister of Defense like Malik."*

*"Are you kidding?"*

*"You created me just to get revenge, didn't you, sir?"*

*"I really feel honored that you chose me to shuck and jive with."*

*"Am I still a 'Honky'?"*

*"... Rufus turned on the white racists who breathed hotly down his back: he turned defiantly upon them, snatching the noose away from the Ku Klux Klansman and raised his clenched fist, shouting, 'Black power, Black power' ... "*

*"Didn't I ask you not to bring your work home at night?"*

*"His argument was more convincing when I read it in the newspapers."*

*"Go ahead, beat me because you need to vent your Oedipal tensions . . .*
*kick me because you identify me with your father . . ."*

*"Are the cops still harassing our organization?"*

*"But just because you're black doesn't mean . . ."*

*"You are going to meet a tall dark man . . ."*

TIGER
BLACK PANTHER
PD

*"That damn Doctor gave me a Nigger's heart,
a Jew's kidney, a Polack's liver . . ."*

*"Al, we're in trouble. The Chief says we're to be on the lookout for a Negro in a long, dark coat."*

*"I don't know where this sister named Circe came from, but she's got a great sense of humor."*

*"Well, I guess now I'll see if Standard Oil or the Bank of America needs a consultant with a degree in Black History."*

EBONY
GROSS
10,000
COPIES

*"Damnit, I told you people before that Daniel Moynihan doesn't live here anymore!"*

*"The joke's on me, Mr. Brewster. I gave you the wrong prescription."*

*"Honey, are we expecting company?"*

HEY, YOU!

GET DOWN HERE WITH THE REST OF US!

C'MON, YOU HEARD ME!

THERE--ISN'T THAT BETTER?!

*"Once over that line, Whitey, consider yourself to be in the 'New Republic of Africa.'"*

LOST AND FOUND

*"Hey, that 'last' cigarette smells kinda funny."*

*"And all the girls in your secretary pool will just love your new 'Che' look . . . "*

*"Well, actually, we haven't much for a heavy dozens player."*

*"Is a Minister of Defense anything like a den mother?"*

*"Your liberal sense of humor is sickening."*

*"Why won't the Black Panther accept me as the King of the Jungle?"*

THE END
IS NEAR

THE END OF RACISM IS NEAR

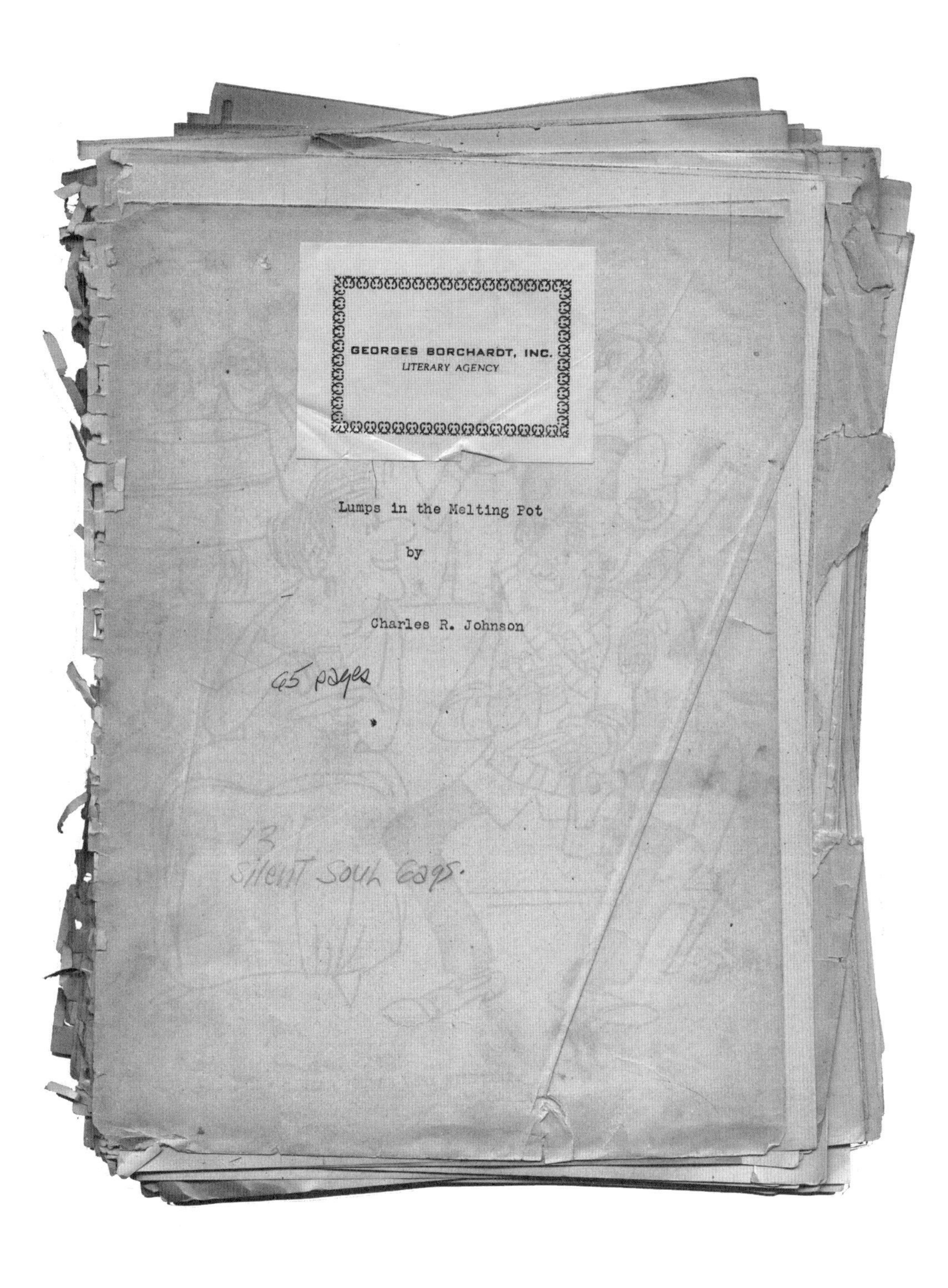
GEORGES BORCHARDT, INC.
LITERARY AGENCY
Lumps in the Melting Pot
by
Charles R. Johnson
65 pages
12
Silent Soul Gaps

# Lumps in the Melting Pot (1973)

In the early 1970s, after *Black Humor* and *Half-Past Nation Time*, I put together a couple more full-length cartoon manuscripts. These would be my last cartoon manuscripts because in 1973, I was fully immersed in novel-writing. I wrote six novels between the years 1970 and 1972, one of them being an early version of *Middle Passage*, while also pursuing graduate work in philosophy.

*Lumps in the Melting Pot* was one of those final cartoon manuscripts. The title was me wondering if "melting pot" had ever been the right metaphor for the black American experience. For the most part, the cartoons in this section continue the themes and tropes I played around with in *Black Humor* and *Half-Past Nation Time,* but they also touch on subjects like the troubled relationship between black people and the police; the depiction of blacks and whites in movies like 1958's *The Defiant Ones*; black people negotiating difficulties in integrated workplaces filled with racial misunderstandings and microaggressions; the laugh-to-avoid-crying experience of poverty; the mind-dulling sameness of some black mass market magazines; more cartoons about militancy; black soldiers in Vietnam; black people at parties; *nouveau riche* black Americans; the Middle Passage, and so forth.

All the original drawings for *Lumps in the Melting Pot* were lost over time and exist only as photocopies which have been miraculously (to me) restored by my publisher, New York Review Comics. It's a joy for me to see them published for the first time. I'm not even sure that I submitted the manuscript anywhere for publication, because the markets I once worked for comic art were starting to disappear in the early 1970s.

These drawings make me reflect on something said once to me by poet and arts activist E. Ethelbert Miller when he interviewed me for a year, which resulted in the book *The Words and Wisdom of Charles Johnson*. He asked me on July 19, 2011, "How does one create good political cartoons without being offensive? When is one man's joke another man's curse? Does laughter bring us together as a community or does it simply reflect the lasting pain of our scars? Are cartoons visual poems?" I devoted two pages to answering his very reasonable questions. And as for his last question? I decided that, yes, a cartoon just possibly might be seen as being a visual poem. Like the best haiku, where a thought or feeling is perfectly expressed in just a few lines and is instantly understood, a well-done cartoon can often lead to an epiphany or "Aha!" moment of laughter and sudden insight into a subject.

"Look moderate."

"So, the Wolf offed the Three Little Pigs and lived happily ever after."

"Kiss me and I'll turn into a virile young W.A.S.P."

"In the book they shot each other."

"Forget your wishes, Whitey, I've got a few demands."

"It's either this, baby, or forty acres and two mules."

NEW
FALL
FASHIONS

"Did you forget—we don't have electricity."

"Prepare for a change of dress and residence."

"Don't worry about promotions, Smith. Just say 'Yassuh, Boss,' to me a few times each day and you'll move up fast."

"I'm willing to try integration if you are, Joe-X."

"We had to find something for them to do."

"*The Saturday Review*, Man. Have you heard of it?"

"Keep punching."

"Johnny, must you taunt the police?"

"I think you'll find, Jackson, that Protagoras meant that all white 'Men are the measure of all things.'"

"All power to the workers."

"Thanks, I've been in the service for ten years."

"Gentlemen, the problem of rats in the ghetto may be solved."

"Rumor has it we've been infiltrated."

"Not bad, Jackson. Just throw in a few more 'Right ons,' and 'Off the Pigs,' and we'll have a best seller."

Chas. Johnson

"That's Joe-X alright."

"He would have wanted it this way."

"I hear you're very militant."

"Shall we tell the Chief that the big one in the beret just taught Mrs. Berenstein how to Bugaloo?"

"Did it ever cross your mind that all these folks might be plain clothesmen?"

"I guess we never will learn who mumbled 'Nigger.'"

"Their thinking we look alike has some advantages."

"I'm worried about Jackson."

"It's not that I don't want to get married—
it's simply that marriage is an archaic white institution—
and we can't participate in that, can we?"

“Jackson!”

"Who's this White Knight I joust with today?"

"Look closer, brother. I'm only passing."

"Sorry, Roscoe, but we're only inviting militants to our parties this year."

"Someday, son, all this will be yours."

"I don't feel like myself at all today, Joan."

"We've just been talking about the death of White Supremacy."

"How long have you been a Black Muslim?"

"Don't start the revolution without me."

"Black Revolution? What Black Revolution?"

"Yeh, Mom, I'm still here in Germany safeguarding freedom and democracy."

post. He was from a town called Fulda, which was about 60 or 75 kilos from our post. It was about 6:00 P.M., but since it was the weekend and we didn't have to work the next day, we decided to make the trip.

We introduced ourselves. His name was Rico. We didn't know at the time that this post was the main power of the KKK Organization, but we found this out shortly after we arrived there. Yes, they were there, and all over. They even had some sort of card to identify themselves with. Fulda was the hell-hole of all the kasernes. The brothers there didn't only have to fight the KKK's, but the officers and uncle toms as well.

We later began to make the trip back to our own kaserne. We were all high, and feeling good about all that we had accomplished in one day. But after returning to for three months. Then they branded me. I was a drug addict, a trouble maker, a militant, a pusher and an active leader for a black social group. They put me out of the company and sent me to a rehabilitation unit.

But here I started receiving all kinds of undue punishment. I was threatened by my 1st Sgt. Then I was at it again, trying to evade all reality. I started going A.W.O.L., saying what I felt to people, and I even fought my 1st Sgt. He kept calling me a no good nigger, a black bastard and a number of other things. I went A.W.O.L. one last time, right before my unit was to go on a field problem. I was ordered to return to post and come to the field. Well, at first I disobeyed this order. Then I came back to post one day and gave myself up. I gave myself up to a doctor. He was a white captain and a very

# Freelance (1968 – 1975)

In the late '60s and into the '70s, I generally published my cartoons and illustrations in what we called the black press. There were publications such as *Black World* (formerly *Negro Digest*), *Proud* magazine in St. Louis, and a few others. But I published anywhere and everywhere I could—regularly and steadily in my campus newspaper, *The Daily Egyptian*, in *The Southern Illinoisan*, *The Chicago Tribune*, in academic publications for the School of Journalism at Southern Illinois University, and one called *Scholastic Editor/Communications and Graphics* in which I published my first article with illustrations, "Creating the Political Cartoon" (1973). I also did the design for a southern Illinois commemorative stamp; illustrations for an outfit in New York that asked me to do drawings of Langston Hughes's character Jesse B. Semple; cartoon work in Dario Politella's *The Illustrated Anatomy of Campus Humor* (1971), and a cartoon self-portrait for *Self-Portrait: Book People Picture Themselves, From the Collection of Burt Britton* (1976). All of this work, and more, is in my papers or literary archive at Washington University in St. Louis: fifty-seven years of comic art, literary and philosophical writings, screenplays, and teleplays.

As one might suspect, freelancing as a black cartoonist isn't the easiest way to be a breadwinner supporting a wife and child, both of which I had by 1975, when I was still a doctoral student. And so my creative energies shifted from drawing to my first and only academic post at the University of Washington, where I concentrated my time on teaching black American literature and creative writing.

*"Wouldn't it have been easier to just close our eyes when they showed Birth of A Nation?"*

*"... And finally, we don't like your obviously elitist attitude."*

*"Another six points off for that turn signal, Jackson."*

*"African look? I thought it was unisex!"*

*"No wonder they can keep their prices so low."*

*"Welcome, welcome!"*

*"That's why I never take a lunch break."*

*"Daddy, come here quick!"*

*"Your militancy is beautiful, but you've got to stop putting George Washington Carver on these singles."*

*"When he said he was for community control, I never guessed..."*

*"And just WHAT'S so terrible about Junior's mixed dating?"*

"...SO MARCUS GARVEY BEAT THE MAIL FRAUD RAP, MOVED ALL US BLACK FOLKS TO AFRICA AND WE ALL LIVED HAPPILY EVER AFTER!"

LOANS
PROBLEMS
DREAMS DEFERRED

"Yeah? Well I say my coiffure is prettier than your coiffure!"

*"Della was so delighted that my new will sets her free that she's gone out to get us a cup of tea."*

*"And who is the Blackest of Them All?"*

*"It's unanimous, Ed—we'd like to hear you do a chorus of 'Old Man River.'"*

*"...Real sad story, he insured all the Black Panthers before they got big."*

*"If you're going home to Africa, then I'm going home to Mother."*

*"How long you been in, old timer?"*

*"You can collect your severance pay, Jones!"*

SHINE
10¢
FANON
POLITICAL
ORIENTATION
25¢
Chas.
Johnson

"Remember: 'Sticks and stones may break my bones...'"

*"Just lay low until after the election, Frank."*

*"Could I hear some of your soul music?"*

*"My, I'll bet your guerillas had a rough day."*

*"Hello, desk? It's about the roaches..."*

*"No offense, Frank, but I don't think we want to wife swap."*

X LOVES Z
KORAN
Chas. Johnson

*"Sarge, do you remember the good old days when we could patrol the ghetto without being patrolled?"*

*"Personally, I don't think a black home should be without one."*

*"We've seen enough of this nonsense. Let's go, Joe."*

*"Maybe we should leave it."*

*"'Take a letter, Miss Simmons... 'Dear Grand Dragon'..."*

HAIRCUTS $5.00
SHAVE
BLACK CULTURE
INTEGRATION
REVOLUTION

"I like you, you're different..."

*"Bet you two to one the little Muslim gets possession of the corner..."*

*"You landlords got no heart..."*

CHAS.
JOHNSON

"When I say you're racy, Cynthia, I don't mean you're a racist."

*"Got any special rates for a one-way group flight to Algeria?"*

"THE OLD MAN WILL HEAR ABOUT THIS!"

*"Tut, tut, Miss Simmons, you knew I was an old bigot when you took the job..."*

*"Relax, your parole officer just passed."*

*"Pleased to meet you. I'm being treated for a Toussaint L'Ouverture complex."*

*"No, man, you're the blackest of them all."*

*"He's at a very inquisitive age."*

*"Stop serving me at my first mention of Black Power."*

*"We can't go on meeting like this, Sylvia."*

*"Not tonight, honey, I've been integrating all day..."*

*"I'll take my coffee over here in the studio, honey."*

*"Now, does anyone have anything important to say before we start speaking Swahili?"*

*"He'll be up protesting in no time."*

"Been here long?"

USED
CARS
"NOW, IF IT'S POWER YOU PEOPLE REALLY
WANT, HERE'S JUST THE BABY FOR YOU!"

*"Something's wrong with me, Doc, I hate basketball."*

OCCUPATION BY MORE THAN 100 HAPPY SOULS IS BOTH DANGEROUS AND UNLAWFUL
Chas Johnson

*"That took guts, Johnny—calling that Green Beret a pig."*

"Congratulations, Jackson—you're the first black commander of the USS Hornblower..."

DIAL-A-
SLOGAN
Chas.
Johnson

*"Now, what makes you think that no one gives you any respect?"*

"A LITTLE LESS BLACK POWER NEXT TIME, OKAY?"

*"I'd like you to meet my wife and fellow lumpenproletariat."*

*"Man! Now that's White Power!"*

*"What amazes me is that she can spend a whole hour talking when it's a wrong number."*

*"I think he has something to do with the American Dilemma or something like that."*

YOUR... BOSS... IS...... PASSING FOR..... WHITE....

*"Thanks, but I think I'll keep hitching."*

*"According to this news bulletin, a new nuclear power must be acknowledged—in Harlem."*

*"Take you to my leader? How? Malcolm's dead, Martin's dead, Rap's in jail, Eldridge in exile..."*

*"All your racial problems will soon end..."*

**LIT CRIT** ***by Charles Johnson***

"Believe me, Richard , I've been in publishing for thirty years and I can assure you, a book about black anger will simply never sell..."

# Later Work (1975 – Present)

In 1990, when my novel *Middle Passage* received the National Book Award in fiction, I was inundated with the business of the literary book world, something that's still true today.

Only a few editors have inquired about the time I spent as a cartoonist. I was always grateful for their interest and leaped at every opportunity to draw something new. For a time, I drew a feature devoted to humor about writers for *Literal Latte*, a free publication in New York City. Other regular markets for a while were *Black Issues in Higher Education* and *Quarterly Black Review*.

A special issue of *African American Review* (winter 1996) devoted to my work contains a large section of my comic art, as do the books *Humor Me: An Anthology of Humor By Writers of Color* (2002), edited by John McNally; *First Words: Earliest Writing From Favorite Contemporary Authors* (1993), edited by Paul Mandelbaum; and Donald Friedman's sublime *The Writer's Brush: Paintings, Drawings, and Sculpture by Writers* (2007).

Cartoons have also appeared in publications as diverse as *American Book Review* (a cover cartoon for the September/October 2014 issue I guest-edited on children's literature); *The Bulletin of the American Academy of Arts & Sciences* (summer 2010); *Tricycle: The*

*Buddhist Review*, which also published several Zen-themed cartoons in a lovely little book titled *Buddha Laughing* (1999); a two-page comic strip on Bruce Lee called "A Dragon's Tale" in Shary Flenniken's *Seattle Laughs* (1994); and *The Seattle Times,* with four cartoons and an essay celebrating Martin Luther King's birthday (January 18, 2004). This listing of recent publications is, of course, not exhaustive.

It's also worth saying that when no opportunities to draw came from others during this winter season of my life, I would make up assignments for myself, as I did in my youth. A recent example are the illustrations I've done for three young adult books in *The Adventures of Emery Jones, Boy Science Wonder* series—*Bending Time*, *The Hard Problem*, and *The Tomorrow No One Wanted*—that I co-authored with my artist daughter Elisheba. The title character is named after my grandson, who draws every day.

*"The best we can figure, Mrs. Reed, is that your husband Ishmael accidentally summoned the Loas and they took him away."*

*"I guess it's not easy to be a black female prof on campus these days."*

*"Whatever you do, son, try not to let anyone know our family has only been white for the last 100 years."*

*"Do you think there's a chance we can turn this into recipes for a bestselling cookbook?"*

Chas. Johnson
"OH, NO, WE DON'T WANT TO MEET YOUR LEADER. WE JUST CAME FOR THE OCTAVIA BUTLER BOOK PARTY!"

*"Oh, maybe I should have told you not to mention Spike Lee or Toni Morrison."*

*"That's as close as this university gets to multiculturalism."*

OH, LORD, I HOPE HE TURNS OUT ALL RIGHT...
HIMES
HAMMETT
CHRISTIE
SPILLANE
CHANDLER
CONAN DOYLE
"MRS MOSLEY, I'M NOT SURE IT'S SUCH A GOOD IDEA FOR LITTLE WALTER TO SPEND SO MUCH TIME READING CRIME FICTION..."

*"Okay, this week we're discussing Charles Johnson's* Dreamer.
*Do you all have your dictionaries ready?"*

*"All I know is that too much one-pointedness can make you really tired."*

*"All right, you can fast longer than me."*

*"What's wrong with you? Dorothy's son reached enlightenment; Janice's son reached enlightenment; Sophia's son..."*

*"Do you have cards of congratulations for those who have just attained enlightenment?"*

*"You sure you got the right retreat?"*

*“Om… om.… om.… om.… om.… om.…”*

*"How can I conquer my ego?"*

*"Sorry, kid, I direct all questions about string theory to him."*

# Acknowledgements

For me, it is simply miraculous that creative work I did so very long ago, almost as if it was in another lifetime (with some of it I can't even remember doing), can experience rebirth in this handsome volume from New York Review Comics. So naturally I am eager to thank my superb editor Lucas Adams, whose passion for this project and indefatigable work in restoring some of these drawings struck me as being phenomenal, indeed, almost magical. I would also like to express my deepest gratitude for the numerous editors since my teens who gave me the opportunity to pursue my earliest passion—drawing—and have my work appear in their publications. I feel equally grateful to Dan Nadel, who featured my comic art in *It's Life As I See It: Black Cartoonists in Chicago 1940–1980*, and the Museum of Contemporary Art Chicago for including my work in their 2021 exhibition, *Chicago Comics: 1960s to Now*.

OF ALL THE THINGS
THAT
DRIVE MEN TO SEA, THE MOST
COMMON DISASTER, I'VE COME
TO LEARN IN MY CASE IT WAS A SPIRITED BOSTON
SCHOOL TEACHER NAMED ISADORA BAILEY BOTH
GREEN TOOK HIS ONE-HORSE RIG INTO TOWN
HE RETURNED
MY CREDITORS I
ISADORA AND
WITH A BONDSMAN NAMED
MUST ADD WHO ENTERED INTO
BUT WHAT LIE AHEAD IN
MINGO IT IS TIME TO TELL
A TRAP A SCHEME A CONSPIRACY SO
AFRICA THEN LATER ON THE OPEN, ENG
LESS SEA WAS A FORTUNE FAR STRANGER
THAN THE ONE I FLED IN NEW ORLEANS
YOU'D FAITH
LONG MY FATHER AND I
WERE SERVANTS IN SOUTH CA-
ROLINA ON A PLANTATION NAMED
CRIPPLEGATE GOD WILLING I
AM GOING TO TELL YOU A
LOVE STORY ME AND MY BR-
OTHER LOFTIS CAME
THROUGH THE
THE OLD
LADIES
Chas. Johnson
HOBBES
THE ART OF MEDITATION
LOGICAL POSITIVISM
SUDDEN FICTION
YOGA

# Also by Charles Johnson

FICTION
*Night Hawks: Stories*
*Dr. King's Refrigerator and Other Bedtime Stories*
*Soulcatcher and Other Stories*
*Dreamer*
*Middle Passage*
*The Sorcerer's Apprentice*
*Oxherding Tale*
*Faith and the Good Thing*

NON-FICTION
*Grand: A Grandparent's Wisdom for a Happy Life*
*The Way of the Writer: Reflections on the Art and Craft of Storytelling*
*The Words and Wisdom of Charles Johnson*
*Taming the Ox: Buddhist Stories and Reflections on Politics, Race, Culture, and Spiritual Practice*
*Passing the Three Gates: Interviews with Charles Johnson (edited by Jim McWilliams)*
*Turning the Wheel: Essays on Buddhism and Writing*
*King: The Photobiography of Martin Luther King Jr. (with Bob Adelman)*
*I Call Myself An Artist: Writings by and about Charles Johnson (edited by Rudolph P. Byrd)*
*Africans in America: America's Journey through Slavery (with Patricia Smith)*
*Black Men Speaking (with John McCluskey Jr.)*

PHILOSOPHY
*Philosophy: An Innovative Introduction: Fictive Narrative, Primary Texts, and Responsive Writing (with Michael Boylan)*
*Being and Race: Black Writing Since 1970*

CARTOONS
*Half-Past Nation Time*
*Black Humor*
*The Eightfold Path (with Steven Barnes and Bryan Moss)*

CHILDREN'S FICTION
*The Adventures of Emery Jones, Boy Science Wonder: The Tomorrow No One Wanted (with Elisheba Johnson)*
*The Adventures of Emery Jones, Boy Science Wonder: Bending Time (with Elisheba Johnson)*
*The Adventures of Emery Jones, Boy Science Wonder: The Hard Problem (with Elisheba Johnson)*

DR. CHARLES JOHNSON, University of Washington (Seattle) professor emeritus and the author of 26 books, is a novelist, philosopher, essayist, literary scholar, short-story writer, cartoonist, illustrator, author of children's literature, and a screen-and-teleplay writer. A 1998 MacArthur fellow, Johnson has received a 2002 American Academy of Arts and Letters Award in Literature, a 1990 National Book Award for his novel *Middle Passage*, a 1985 Writers Guild Award for his PBS teleplay *Booker*, the 2016 W.E.B. Du Bois Award at the National Black Writers Conference, and many other honors. Johnson's most recent publications are *The Way of the Writer: Reflections on the Art and Craft of Storytelling*; *Night Hawks: Stories*; *Grand: A Grandparent's Wisdom for a Happy Life*; and with Steven Barnes, he is co-author of the forthcoming graphic novel *The Eightfold Path*.

# ALSO AVAILABLE FROM NEW YORK REVIEW COMICS

YELLOW NEGROES AND OTHER IMAGINARY CREATURES
Yvan Alagbé

PIERO
Edmond Baudoin

ALMOST COMPLETELY BAXTER
Glen Baxter

AGONY
Mark Beyer

MITCHUM
Blutch

PEPLUM
Blutch

THE GREEN HAND AND OTHER STORIES
Nicole Claveloux

WHAT AM I DOING HERE?
Abner Dean

THE TENDERNESS OF STONES
Marion Fayolle

TROTS AND BONNIE
Shary Flenniken

LETTER TO SURVIVORS
Gébé

PRETENDING IS LYING
Dominique Goblet

VOICES IN THE DARK
Ulli Lust

ALAY-OOP
William Gropper

ELEPHANT *AND* THE PROJECTOR
Martin Vaughn James

W THE WHORE
Anke Feuchtenberger and Katrin de Vries

JIMBO: ADVENTURES IN PARADISE
Gary Panter

FATHER AND SON
E.O. Plauen

SOFT CITY
Pushwagner

THE NEW WORLD
Chris Reynolds

PITTSBURGH
Frank Santoro

DISCIPLINE
Dash Shaw

MACDOODLE ST.
Mark Alan Stamaty

SLUM WOLF
Tadao Tsuge

THE MAN WITHOUT TALENT
Yoshiharu Tsuge

RETURN TO ROMANCE
Ogden Whitney